Dick King-Smith

Poppet

Illustrated by Mike Terry

PUFFIN BOOKS

PUFFIN BOOKS

Published by the Penguin Group
Penguin Books Ltd, 80 Strand, London WC2R 0RL, England
Penguin Group (USA) Inc., 375 Hudson Street, New York, New York 10014, USA
Penguin Group (Canada), 90 Eglinton Avenue East, Suite 700, Toronto, Ontario, Canada M4P 2Y3
(a division of Pearson Penguin Canada Inc.)
Penguin Ireland, 25 St Stephen's Green, Dublin 2, Ireland (a division of Penguin Books Ltd)
Penguin Books Australia Ltd, 707 Collins Street, Melbourne, Victoria 3008, Australia
(a division of Pearson Australia Group Pty Ltd)
Penguin Books India Pvt Ltd, 11 Community Centre, Panchsheel Park, New Delhi – 110 017, India
Penguin Group (NZ), 67 Apollo Drive, Rosedale, North Shore 0632, New Zealand
(a division of Pearson New Zealand Ltd)
Penguin Books (South Africa) (Pty) Ltd, Block D, Rosebank Office Park, 181 Jan Smuts Avenue,
Parktown North, Gauteng 2193, South Africa

Penguin Books Ltd, Registered Offices: 80 Strand, London WC2R 0RL, England

puffinbooks.com

First published in *More Animal Stories* by Puffin Books 1999
Published in this edition 1999

021

Text copyright © Fox Busters Ltd, 1999
Illustrations copyright © Mike Terry, 1999
All rights reserved

The moral right of the author and illustrator has been asserted

Printed in China

British Library Cataloguing in Publication Data
A CIP catalogue record for this book is available from the British Library

ISBN 978-0-141-30264-5

··· Chapter One ···

When Poppet was born, he had absolutely no idea what sort of animal he was.

He looked around, and saw that he was surrounded by a forest of legs. Huge legs they were, thick and tall and greyish in colour, with huge feet on the end of them.

Poppet looked up, and saw, on

top of all those legs, huge bodies with huge heads and huge ears and amazingly long, long noses.

He was in fact looking up at his mother, and a number of his aunties who had all come along to inspect this new baby.

"Oh!" said one auntie. "Isn't he a poppet!"

The baby's mother looked extremely pleased.

"What are you going to call him?" said another auntie.

The baby's mother, whose own name was Ooma, said, "I don't know, I haven't had time to think," and then she thought for a bit, and then she said, "But now I do know.

I'll call him Poppet." And she put the tip of her trunk against one of the baby's ears and whispered, "Hello, baby. I'm your mum, and your name is Poppet."

Poppet looked up at Ooma and the other huge animals and said, "Please, what sort of animals are you?"

"Elephants," said Ooma. "We are African elephants."

"Oh," said Poppet. "But you said you were my mum."

"Yes."

"So does that make me an African elephant?"

"Yes."

Poppet looked puzzled. There must be some mistake, he thought.

"You're enormous," he said, "and I'm very small. We can't be the same sort of animal."

"Oh yes we are," said Ooma. "It's just that you're a baby elephant."

"But you'll grow," said one of the aunties.

"And grow," said another.

"And grow."

"And grow."

"And grow," said all the others.

"Until you're as big as we are," said Ooma. "You might even be bigger one day."

"Tomorrow?" said Poppet.

At this, the aunties all laughed

quietly, making snuffly noises in their trunks, before moving slowly and heavily away, leaving mother and baby alone together.

··· Chapter Two ···

"**N**o, not tomorrow, Poppet," said Ooma gently.
"Elephants take a long, long time to grow to full size. But you'll get there one day. There's nothing to stop you, for we are too big and our skins are too thick for any other creature in Africa to hurt us. Except two."

"What are they, Mum?" asked Poppet.

"One," said Ooma, "is a monkey-like thing called a man. Men kill elephants."

"Why?"

"For their tusks."

"What are tusks?"

"Great big long teeth that elephants have. Like these two of mine."

"I haven't got any."

"You will. But you should be all right, because we live in a special place called a reserve, where elephants are protected."

"Oh," said Poppet. "But you said there were *two* creatures that could hurt us. What's the other one, besides a man?"

"A mouse," said Ooma.

"Oh," said Poppet. "Are they even bigger and stronger than us, these mouses?"

"Mice," said Ooma, "are very small and, what's more, mice live in holes, and that's the trouble."

She stretched out her long, long trunk till the tip of it was right in front of Poppet's face.

"What do you see, Poppet?" she said.

"A hole," said Poppet.

Then Ooma, speaking slowly and solemnly, repeated to her newborn child the old elephant-wives' tale that her mother had told her when she was a baby, a tale in which she had always believed.

"Poppet, my son," she said.

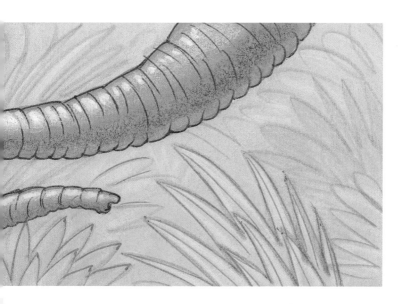

"First, never have anything to do with mice. Second, if you should be unfortunate enough to meet one, keep your trunk curled up out of the way. Never, never put the tip of it anywhere near a mouse, otherwise the most dreadful thing imaginable will happen to you."

"What's that?" said Poppet.

"The mouse will run up the inside of your trunk."

··· Chapter Three ···

Poppet thought about this for the rest of the first day of his life.

He imagined this thing called a mouse running along inside his little trunk and he did not like the thought of it at all. Suppose one did! How would he get rid of it? Blow it out, he supposed, and every so often, for the rest of the day,

he blew very hard, suddenly, down his trunk, just in case one of the awful creatures had somehow crept in.

I don't even know what they look like, he thought, only that they're small.

The next morning, while the elephant herd was browsing upon the leaves of some large trees, Poppet was standing beside his mother when he saw a strange animal moving about on the bark of one of the trees.

What it was he didn't know, but it was certainly small.

Carefully curling his trunk up out of harm's way, Poppet bent his head towards it. Close up, he could see that the creature, though small, was long, with a great many joints to its dark brown body and a very great many legs.

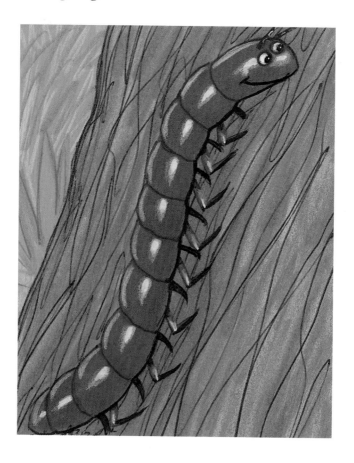

Perfect for crawling up elephants' trunks, he thought. I bet you are one.

He said politely, "Excuse me, but are you a mouse?"

"A mouse?" said the creature.

"Yes. I thought you might be."

"You're joking! Pull the other one."

"Other what?"

"Leg."

What does it mean? Poppet thought. It's got hundreds of legs. "Well, if you're not a mouse," he said, "what are you?"

"I'm a giant millipede," said the long wriggly creature.

"A giant!" said Poppet.

"Oh, stop taking the mickey,"

said the millipede huffily. "You knew all the time, didn't you? I could tell – I wasn't born yesterday."

"I was," said Poppet, as the giant millipede rippled away.

"But anyway, I've learned something. That animal was not a mouse."

Chapter Four

In the days and weeks that followed, he asked quite a number of small creatures whether they were mice.

He asked beetles and grubs and worms and caterpillars and little lizards and small frogs, and some replied jokily and some replied angrily and some didn't answer.

Till at last Poppet rather forgot
about his mother's dire warning and
gave himself up to enjoying the
carefree life of a baby elephant. He
used his trunk for reaching up and
pulling down leaves and twigs, and
for sucking up water when the herd
went to the river to drink, and then

blowing water all over himself.
When he was nice and wet, he
would go to a dusty place and use
his trunk to give himself a dust-
bath, so that he finished up
beautifully muddy. Then he'd go
back into the river and have a
lovely bathe, going right under the

water, with just the tip of his trunk sticking up above the surface, like a snorkel.

A trunk, Poppet decided, was a brilliant thing to have.

As for mice, he never thought about them any more.

Then one hot afternoon, when he was about a month old, and his mother and all the aunties were standing resting in the shade, Poppet wandered off a little way, exploring.

He was using his trunk to search about in the grass as he went along, when suddenly he saw in front of him an animal that he had not previously met. It was furry and brown, with large tulip-shaped ears,

beady black eyes and a longish hairless tail, and Poppet stretched out his trunk towards it and sniffed at it.

Even when the tip of his trunk was right before the creature's face, it didn't occur to him that this animal was small, and – without much hope because he'd been wrong so many times – he said, "Are you a mouse?"

"As a matter of fact," said the animal, "I am. And you know what mice do to elephants, don't you?"

··· Chapter Five ···

Hastily, Poppet raised his trunk. "Aha!" said the mouse. "Your mum told you, did she?"

"Told me what?"

"That mice run up inside elephants' trunks."

"Well, yes," said Poppet. "She did."

"And you believed her?"

"Yes."

The mouse let out a loud squeak, whether of anger or of fright Poppet did not know (in fact it was of delight).

"What are you called, boy?" it said.

"Poppet. What about you?"

"My name," said the mouse, "is

Momo, and I am very glad to meet you."

"Oh," said Poppet. "Why?"

"Because," said Momo, "when I was very young, my mother told me this story about mice and elephants and I didn't believe her. That's rubbish, I thought. One day, I said to myself, I'll meet an elephant and

find out if it's true. And now I've met one."

"But you're not going to find out," said Poppet, and he curled his trunk even higher.

"Oh, come on!" said Momo. "Be a sport. Just let me have a look up it."

"No, no!" cried Poppet. "You'll crawl in."

"I won't, honest."

"Promise?"

"Cross my heart."

So, very slowly, Poppet uncurled his trunk and lowered the tip of it towards the waiting mouse. The nearer it got to Momo, the more nervous Poppet became.

I must be mad, he thought,

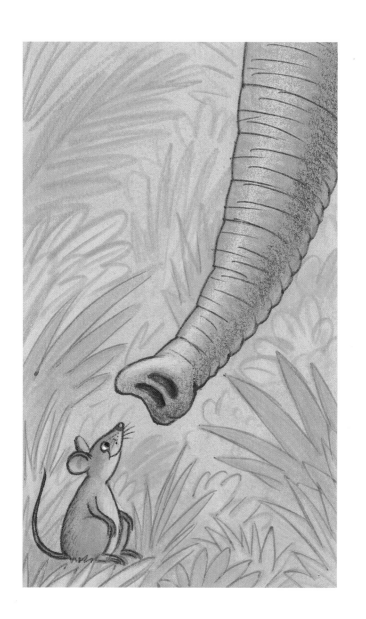

believing a mouse's promise. Mice probably don't know the meaning of the word.

Then suddenly he felt the tickle of whiskers at the very tip of his trunk as Momo peered into it, and he gave an enormous sneeze.

··· Chapter Six ···

Elephants, like people, shut their eyes when they sneeze, and when Poppet opened his again, it was to see that the mouse had been blown head over heels by the force of the blast.

"Steady on!" cried Momo. "What are you playing at?"

"Sorry," said Poppet. "I sneezed."

"Oh. Well, bless you."

"Thanks. It was your whiskers.
They tickled."

"Just testing. A mouse can go into
any hole that's wider than its
whiskers."

"And was it?"

"It would have been a very tight

fit," said Momo. "Might be possible
with a full-grown elephant, but I
shouldn't have cared to try it with
you, Poppet my lad. Anyway, to be
quite frank, it looked pretty damp
and uninviting up there, even before
the sneeze. As it is, I'm soaked."

"I'll dry you," said Poppet, and

he pointed his trunk at the mouse
and blew long slow hot breaths over
him.

It was while he was doing this
that he suddenly heard his mother's
voice, and a very angry voice it was.
Ooma had walked up behind him,
quite silently, as elephants do on
their great cushioned feet, only to
see her son with his trunk
outstretched, the tip of it only
centimetres from a mouse!

She let out a furious trumpet, and
Momo vanished from sight.

"What did I tell you?" screamed
Ooma. "Keep away from mice,
d'you hear me? Get out of my way
now and I'll squash this one flat."

"Oh, don't, Mum!" cried Poppet.

"He's my friend!"

"Your friend!" snorted Ooma.
"You're not just a bad child, you're
a mad child." And she went

stamping about in the grass till
she'd flattened a big patch of it.

"That should have fixed the horrid
creature," she said, and she moved
away to rejoin the herd, grumbling
to herself.

Poppet stood sadly beside the
trampled patch.

"Alas, poor mouse!" he said. "It's all my fault that he's dead."

"No he isn't," said a voice, and out of the grass poked a little brown head, whiskers twitching.

"Momo!" cried Poppet. "You're not hurt?"

"Got a bit of a headache."

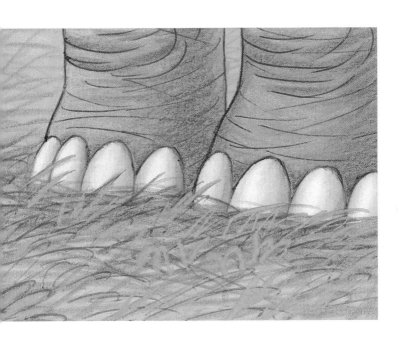

"How on earth did you survive?"

"Under earth. Went down a hole, sharpish," said the mouse. "But not before I heard what you said. Which was nice of you, Poppet. You are my friend too."

··· Chapter Seven ···

Meanwhile, Ooma was telling the aunties about her naughty child.

"One of the first things I told him," she said, "was to keep away from mice. We all know that every mouse is just waiting for a chance to run up the inside of our trunks."

"We do," said the aunties.

"And no doubt you all gave your kids the same warning."

"We did," said the aunties.

"And what have I just found? Only my boy with the tip of his trunk right beside a mouse, that's all. I told him off, I can tell you. No doubt you'd have done the same?"

"We would," said the aunties.

"Children!" said Ooma. "They just don't listen."

"Grown-ups!" said Poppet to Momo at about the same time. "They don't treat children fairly, grown-ups don't. I could have explained to Mum if she'd let me. I could have told her, 'You're wrong. Mice don't run up elephants' trunks. I know. My friend told me.' But no,

I never got the chance. She just yelled at me."

"I heard it," said Momo.

"Let's just hope we're more understanding when we're grown-ups," said Poppet.

"Actually," said Momo, "I'm a grown-up already."

"Oh, sorry! I didn't realize. You're so . . . um . . ."

"Small?"

"Well, yes."

"Tell you what, Poppet," said the mouse. "Do you agree that it would be a good thing if elephants stopped being frightened of mice?"

"Yes, I do."

"And do you agree that it would be a good thing if elephants stopped trying to squash mice?"

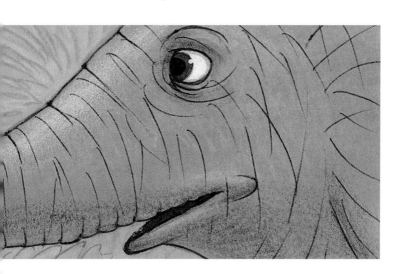

"Oh yes, I do."

"Right then. This is my plan. Listen carefully."

And so it was that later that day, when the herd had been down to the river to bathe and the elephants were all standing in the shade,

resting, Poppet said to Ooma,
"Mum, will you promise not to yell
at me if I tell you something?"

"Of course I won't," said Ooma,
who was already rather ashamed of
losing her temper with her little one.

"Of course you won't promise?"

"No. Of course I won't yell at
you."

"All right then," said Poppet. "It's
this. Mice do *not* run up inside
elephants' trunks. They never have
and they never will."

Ooma snorted.

"Come and listen to this," she
called to the aunties, and when they
had all gathered round, she made
Poppet repeat his words.

"Silly boy," said one auntie, and,

"Stupid child," said another, and a third said, "You had a narrow escape this morning. You might not be so lucky another time."

"Wait here, please," said Poppet, and he disappeared into some bushes. When he emerged again, Ooma and the aunties could see that he was holding something in the tip of his trunk, something furry and brown, with large tulip-shaped ears, beady black eyes and a longish hairless tail – a mouse!

··· Chapter Eight ···

How horrified they all were! They formed a circle around Poppet, their trunks held high out of the reach of the dreaded creature that he carried, and they shifted anxiously from foot to foot, fanning their great ears.

Poppet put the mouse carefully down upon the ground.

"This is Momo," he said to Ooma and the aunties. "My friend, like I told you, Mum. I know I am only a child, but Momo is a grown-up, even though you may think he's not grown very far. However, he has a grown-up brain, I can tell you, and he wishes to address you all, if you will be kind enough to listen to him."

So astonished were the elephants, first to see Poppet carrying the mouse, and then to hear him make such a speech, that they stopped fidgeting and stood, silent, except for the rumbling of their tummies, which they couldn't help.

Momo sat up on his hunkers.

"Ladies," he said. "It is a great

privilege to be allowed to speak to
you, and," he turned to face Ooma,
"especially you, madam, the mother
of a truly remarkable child."

Elephants can't blush, but if
Ooma could have done, she would
have done.

"Poppet," the mouse went on, "is

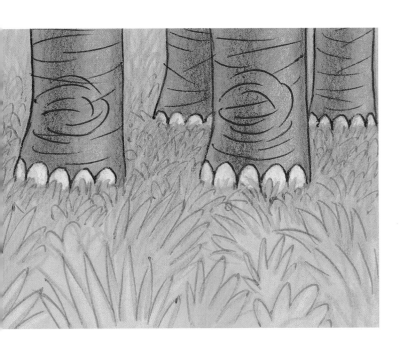

a name that all elephants will
remember for all time, since it is he
– with a little help from myself –
who has been the first of his kind to
discover that mice do *not*, never
have, and never will run up the
inside of elephants' trunks. I call
upon him now to conclude this

historic day by offering to all of you the proof of what I have just said. So that none of you here, indeed none of your kind throughout the length and breadth of Africa, need ever again worry about meeting a mouse, trunk to face. Now Poppet, say your piece."

"Mum," said Poppet. "Do you love me?"

"Oh yes, Poppet," said Ooma.

"Would you do anything for me?"

"Oh yes."

"Then uncurl your trunk and stretch out the tip of it to Momo."

"Oh no, Poppet! I couldn't!"

"Courage, madam," said Momo, while all the aunties cried, "Go on, Ooma!" safe in the knowledge that

they didn't have to do it.

"It'll be all right, Mum," said Poppet. "Honest."

So very slowly, with her eyes tight shut, Ooma uncoiled her trunk and laid the tip of it on the ground, right beside the mouse. Momo peered up it, careful (remembering Poppet's sneeze) not to touch it with his whiskers.

"Yuck!" he said softly.

Then he said to Ooma, "Thank you, madam. I appreciate your confidence and your courage, and I

am filled with admiration for the undoubted beauty, strength and dexterity of your magnificent nasal appendage. I hope, however, that you will forgive me if I say that nothing in this world could ever persuade me to creep up your trunk."

"I had a job to keep a straight

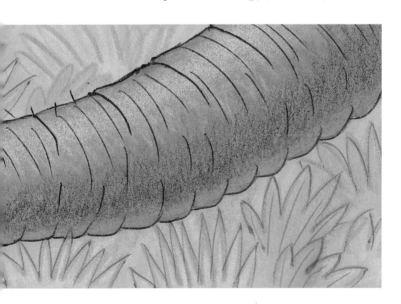

face," said Momo when the herd had moved away, shaking their great heads in wonder at what they had just seen and heard.

Ooma especially seemed quite overcome by what had happened, and when Poppet said to her, "Mum, can I stay and play with Momo?" she answered, "Yes, of course, dear," as though hypnotized.

When they were alone, Poppet said "What shall we play? Can you think of a game?"

"Yes," said Momo. "Put down your trunk and I'll run up it."

"Oh no!" cried Poppet. "You mean it's true after all, what Mum told me? And I thought you were my friend!"

"I am," said Momo. "Don't get your trunk in a twist. I just want to run up the *outside*."